About the Author

John Steinberg spent many years in business before becoming a writer in 2007. Since then, he's co-written and produced comedies for the stage, published five novels, and an illustrated book for adults. Jacob Returns is his first novella. He is married with three children and lives in North London.

JACOB RETURNS

John Steinberg

2QT Limited (Publishing)

First Edition in 2025 by
2QT Limited (Publishing)

Cover design Hilary Pitt,
Cover image is attributed to Safeef /Shutterstock.com

This book is a work of fiction. Any references to historical events, real
people or real places other than those clearly in the public domain, are used
fictitiously. Other names, characters, places, and events are products of the
author's imagination, and any resemblance to actual events or persons, living
or dead, is entirely coincidental.

Printed in the UK by Ingrams Inc (UK)

A CIP catalogue record for this book is available from the British
Library.
ISBN 978-1-0684439-6-1

"If I'm not for myself, who will be for me?

If I'm only for myself, what am I? And if not now, when?"

Hillel

Prologue

North London cemetery

At the end of the short address, a healthy gathering of mourners accompanied the plain wooden coffin of the much-admired Morris Barnet as it was wheeled out of the old stone chapel with Miles Davis's haunting 'Kinda Blue', playing softly in the background.

The fact that it was deemed suitable to go for a formal ceremony, albeit a nondenominational one, was a surprise for most of the attendees who knew from personal experience that religion had played no part in their mentor's life.

Unlike so many, this was a person who was never prepared to leave anything to chance. For Morris Barnet there were no unresolvable questions, just a deficiency of knowledge to determine their answers.

Up to and until the last moment, there was little evidence from the regular stream of visitors he continued to receive at his Hampstead home that there was anything awry. Other than a persistent cough, which was dismissed out of hand as a heavy cold, and that the front door of the elegant Georgian abode in which, apart from his devoted housekeeper, Joan, he'd lived alone, was left permanently ajar, nothing seemed immediately amiss.

Morris had always been elusive about his private life. Although he'd occasionally let slip a hint of the existence of a family, no one actually believed it, putting it down instead to some skewed desire for normality. But there'd been nothing normal about the jazz-loving figure. In his beret and thick, black-framed glasses, he resembled a member of Paris's Left Bank Avant-Garde of the 1960s. At least that was the image he portrayed at the university where he taught his unique brand of rationalism, careful to avoid any reference to the privileged background from which he actually derived, which might have damaged his persona. The author of dozens of papers on the power of the individual attracted a cult following of young people ready to disregard the traditional views of their parents in favour of handing over the shaping of their lives to someone, instead, who appealed more to their anarchic instincts.

The cortege slowly made its way along an uneven path, picking up more people as it proceeded on its final journey, coming to a halt ten minutes later, at a freshly dug grave.

Suddenly, a flamboyant young man dressed head to toe in black, his face obscured by a designer stubble and matching wrap-round sunglasses, pushed his way to the front.

'Make way! Make way!' he boomed in a broad Irish accent and, oblivious to the looks he'd provoked, picked up a shovel and began filling in the grave.

'Just like the fella grabbing the limelight all to himself,' he muttered as if he was merely staking his claim. Then, when he'd fulfilled his task, he just thrust the implement back into the earth and walked briskly away with no one the wiser as to his true identity.

Remaining behind long after the last mourners had dispersed, contemplating the loss of a remarkable person and the void he'd left in so many of their lives, the same individual reclined on a nearby bench, flipping through the order of service he'd just witnessed.

'This has to be some different fella,' he said to himself with an irresponsible expression, suggesting he was in possession of some unique insight into the emeritus professor to which no one else had been privy. Granting the tribute a more detailed look, the thought suddenly occurred to him: *what if he'd been too dismissive of its contents and it portrayed a more accurate reflection of the father that he, Jacob Barnet, had always imagined?*

Perhaps it was partly that unconscious desire that had brought him here when he had all the justification in the world to forget the man had ever existed. Suddenly, he was consumed by an urgent need to establish whether there was more to the person he'd just helped bury than he'd imagined.

1

Later that afternoon, Jacob arrived at the nearby residential street in earshot of Golders Green Station. It was easy enough to locate the details of the man behind the lectern. Jangling his mythical lost bunch of keys in front of the old beadle, whom he'd found loitering behind the prayer hall, was all it had taken for the gullible fellow to rummage around for details of its owner. Not that the name, Simon Freedman, resonated in any particular way, indistinguishable amongst the lugubrious throng similarly taken in by the charismatic academic to whom they'd come to pay their respects.

Wiping from his mouth the remnants of the ploughman's he'd stopped for on the way, he made his presence felt with a loud thump on the outside of a pebble-dashed semi that had fallen into disrepair with flaking paint on the window frames and several missing slates from the roof. It amused him to speculate what if the run-down abode belonged, instead, to a stooge they hired just for the day because they couldn't find anyone else to say a good word about the recently deceased?

A few moments later, a short grey-haired man in a crumpled suit appeared at the door.

'Hello, can I help you?' he asked.

'Well, isn't that the sixty-four thousand dollar question?' Jacob replied.

'I'm sorry, I don't think I know you. My name's Simon

Freedman; maybe you've got me mixed up with someone else?'

He was about to close the door when Jacob countered, 'More to the point is who *you* might be to spout out all that blarney about old Morris here?' He prodded at the front-page image of the service programme as if the person to whom he was referring was simply conspicuous by his absence.

It took a moment for the situation to fully register before the older man could muster a response.

'Yes, yes of course, please accept my apologies for not remembering you amongst all those people. Please do come in,' Freedman blustered, trying to amend for his error.

'It was quite a send-off considering the nature of the beast, unless the turnout was because they were glad to see the back of the fella,' Jacob postulated, stepping into the house, a musty odour pervading the air in keeping with its tired-looking interior.

'If you'd care to follow me, I've got a bit of time till my next patient,' the first man said, leading the way up the stairs to a space the size of a narrow second bedroom with the only natural light provided by a small bank of leaded glass windows at either end. Apart from a few scattered pieces of furniture, wall-to-wall books covered most of the remaining carpeted area.

'Do make yourself comfortable,' he requested, settling back behind an old mahogany desk piled high with cardboard files.

'So, would I be right in thinking you'd be a medical man of sorts?' Jacob enquired, pulling up one of the pair of slatted dining chairs allocated to visitors.

'Is it really that obvious?' the other person remarked, light-heartedly.

'Threw a googly with that lay preacher bit then?' Jacob replied.

'The role was rather imposed upon me,' the first one disclosed.

'And very convincing you were too, up in front of all those people in your Sunday best. Who would have guessed it was only a side-line?'

'Actually, I'm a psychotherapist,' Freedman divulged.

'Well, there's a surprise for you. Though the works on Freud and Jung are a bit of a giveaway,' Jacob replied, showing a particular interest in the volumes nearest to where he was sitting. 'I've always wondered what it'll be like sitting here with one of you fellas.'

'Oh, and why might that be?' the therapist asked.

'Finding out more about yourself—what makes you do certain things? That is what you do, isn't it?'

'It's more about dealing with deep-seated problems of identity.'

'Now there's the thing, the person behind the façade. Shouldn't imagine there's any shortage of takers,' Jacob quipped. 'Just makes the whole thing with Morris here all the more intriguing, wouldn't you say?'

'I gather then, you had a special relationship with Morris Barnet,' the therapist replied.

'That's one way of putting it, though I'm not sure being disowned by one's father falls under that category.'

There was no response, just the therapist giving the impression he was absorbing what had been revealed.

'So, this has all come as a bit of a surprise, has it?' Jacob said picking up on the other man's pensive disposition.

'There was never any real indication that Morris ever had a family,' the therapist replied, choosing his words with care.

'Knowing who we're dealing with here, it's pretty safe to assume he never went about advertising the fact. But with you obviously having a completely different take on the man, I thought it'd be interesting to compare notes.'

'You're referring to the relationship between you and your father?'

'He abrogated *that* position a long time ago,' Jacob divulged.

'And there was no contact between you?'

'Not much, although, to give the man some credit, he coughed up the odd quid or two whenever his conscience got the better of him.'

'I assume you mean for your mother and yourself?'

Jacob nodded. 'Although, who knows? It wouldn't surprise me if Morris had other skeletons in the cupboard just waiting to stake their claim.'

'Yet, you chose to keep his name, which is interesting.'

'Is that your way of trying to gain some deep psychological insight into one of your patients?,' Jacob retorted.

'Sorry, old habits die hard…Tell me how you think I can help you?' the therapist enquired, becoming conscious of the time.

'Finding out more about your man, Morris, and what drove him to do what he did, might be a good start.'

The therapist pondered for a moment then, 'Seems that you're better placed to make that assumption. So, why don't you begin by filling in the gaps.'

Jacob flinched. Suddenly, finding himself under the

spotlight wasn't on the agenda. If he didn't recover the initiative fast, he'd best be on his way; not an easy call when he was so churned up inside!... Then, as if he'd suddenly forfeited his freedom of action, he just leaned back on his chair and started to recount how Morris Barnet first came into their lives more than thirty years before, the intimate relationship he formed with a female student, named Cara Hogan in 1972, and the extent of its subsequent cover-up.

'The whole faculty knew what he was up to and yet were prepared to shut its eyes!' Jacob continued.

'Perhaps the university assessed his reputation was such that it was worth protecting,' the therapist replied.

'A decision purely based on self-interest?' Jacob surmised.

'Morris, sorry your father *was* quite a personality.'

'So, you're saying a bit of tittle-tattle wouldn't have done him any harm?'

'An interesting supposition, and one which may have been complicated by the fact there was a child involved?' the therapist replied.

'Not from Morris's standpoint,' Jacob countered, re-asserting himself.

'Are you implying that your mother hoped they had a future together?'

'A young girl of nineteen, fresh off the boat from County Cork? Morris was her first serious relationship; of course she did.' A sly expression appearing on his handsome face. 'What you need to understand is that my mother was no ordinary student. As his star pupil, she thought she was top of the charts.'

'So, what happened?'

'Your man Morris tried to buy us off with a ticket back

to Ireland and washed his hands of the whole thing.'

'But he must have known about the baby?'

'The birth was complicated, leading to an extended absence from university,' repeating the story he'd always been given.

'And what was Morris's reaction to all this?'

'He was supportive, at first, but the longer the recovery the better it suited him. The university had all but forgotten about his indiscretion and in turn he did the same to us.'

'So, how did you cope? It must have been extremely difficult,' the therapist sympathised.

'It was fortunate my mother's family gathered around and helped her find her feet. Strangely, non-judgmental for a bunch of Irish Catholics!'

'But you said she left university before she completed her degree?'

'It was a foregone conclusion that she'd be awarded a first,' Jacob explained.

'Which enabled her to get a position doing what exactly?'

'A little bit of this and a little bit of that. Then, she got a teaching job away at a secondary school in Dublin.'

'It can't have been easy for you,' the therapist sympathised.

'Growing up not knowing who you really are; you could say that.'

'Sounds very much like you were left to your own devices.'

'That's what a spell in Oberstown detention centre does for you. To be fair, three-square meals a day and a roof over your head, the place was a step up from what I was used to.' Jacob skated over the chill that ran down his spine, alone in the dock of the local magistrate's court when he was cruelly handed down a two-year sentence. He could still hear the sound of the metal door being slammed shut and bolted each night in the cramped cell he shared with the unpredictably violent Paddy O'Leary. Looking back, how he got through those first weeks was nothing short of a miracle.

'For doing what? If you don't mind me asking.'

'A bit of dealing drugs here and there, nothing major but it helped put food on the table while I was still at college.'

'And your mother. Didn't she suspect what you were up to?'

'We didn't have the easiest of relationships. She saw too much of Morris in me for comfort and, in turn, I suppose I blamed her for my existence.'

'Did she meet anyone else after Morris? After all, she was still a young woman.'

'There were a few she was sweet on, but nothing came of them.' A wide smirk appeared on Jacob's face indicating he wouldn't have been averse to sabotaging the chances of anything developing further.

There was a short pause then, 'It's not beyond the realms of possibility your mother was looking for your approval,' the therapist surmised.

'My head wasn't in a good place, so the easiest thing was to lash out…surely you can see that?'

'Retaliatory action against those we're closest to isn't uncommon,' the older man remarked.

'Reverting to your usual role again and when we've only just got going!' Jacob tutted. 'Next you're telling me we're out of time!' he added, glancing at the wooden mantel clock taking a prominent position on the desk in front of him. 'You need to understand, it was all about trying to find out who I really was. So, I created different personas until I found one that fitted,' Jacob continued.

'How long were you detained?' the therapist enquired.

'Long enough to realise that I had no one else to depend on other than myself.'

'But it appears you came out of the experience intact.'

'Put it this way, it enabled me to pick up where I left off with my studies and develop my penmanship skills. I ended up being the main contributor to that place's magazine, for my sins.' Jacob didn't mention the ignominy of the electronic ankle tag he was forced to wear as a condition of his six-month probation or subsequently the number of doors slammed in his face even over the most menial of jobs.

'So, you knew what you wanted to do from early on,' the therapist continued.

'At first, it was an escape route from what I'd missed out on. Then, the more I got into it, the more I found out about myself through the characters I'd invented.'

'So, you're a writer?'

'Freelance for the *Cork Independent*. It doesn't pay that well. My partner works, so it keeps the wolf from the door.'

'At what? Might I ask?'

'Kayleigh's a pharmacist, which is useful – me being bit of a hypochondriac! Come to think of it, she'd be more than happy to oblige with my prescription when we're done.' Jacob winked.

The therapist forced a smile.

'And we still haven't got to talking about the main man. Who was the real Morris Barnet behind the mask? And more relevantly, why did he nominate you to extol his virtues?'

'Maybe we can leave that for another occasion,' the therapist proposed, conscious of the time of his next appointment. 'How long are you in London?'

'I've an open ticket back to the Emerald Isle,' Jacob replied. 'Apparently, Morris left some sort of last will, so that solicitor fella claimed who tracked me down. Did you not already know that?' Jacob said, getting up from his chair. He wasn't going to divulge the fact he already knew he'd been named in the wretched thing. As far as he was concerned, the sooner he got his hands on whatever was due to him, the sooner he'd be on the first ferry back home, hopefully that much richer from when he arrived.

'Perhaps we can meet again if you think it's worthwhile,' was all the therapist said, handing across his business card. He then showed Jacob Barnet to the door, which was met with no more than a non-committal shrug as the younger man strode unaccompanied down the stairs. A few moments later, there was the sound of the front door closing behind him.

Jacob strode disconsolately away with more questions than answers when it should have been the other way around. Whether he should cut his losses, he'd decide over a few drinks in the pub, a few miles away, where he was destined to spend a second night.

2

The next evening, Jacob sent a text message to the therapist saying he was on his way back over to the house in Golders Green. His natural impetuousness had eventually given way to a clearer head telling him that since he had to stick around for a while longer, there were worse ways than taking up the man, Freedman's, offer by gracing him with his presence. He wasn't yet aware, it was purely a cover for the pursuit of an identity he'd been deprived of.

Thirty minutes later, seated around the kitchen table, overnight case by his side, Jacob revealed the circumstances behind the late-night visit.

'Here's me thinking if the man Simon puts me up for a while, we might be able to get to know each other a little better,' he said, concluding his tale of how he'd found Morris Barnet's Hampstead abode chained and boarded up, when he arrived from the train station.

'There's this pair of swarmy estate agent boys on the pavement arguing the toss as to who had the sales instructions on the place,' he continued. 'Attracted quite a crowd, I can tell you. Probably thought it was a film set and they'd get a gig as extras once the cameras started rolling. From what I managed to overhear, when Morris departed this world, the property reverted to the freeholders.'

'So, you're saying that he only ever had a lease on the place?' the therapist queried.

'Sitting tenants was the term I think they used.'

'And there was the housekeeper. She'd been with Morris for years. Must have seen the writing on the wall because there was no one else there. Fortunately, I found a bed for the night, nearby. A few whisky chasers to calm the old nerves did the trick. Nearly missed the old fella's finest hour, I was so out for the count!' He laughed out loud.

'And the contents of the house?' the therapist enquired.

'A couple of haulage lorries were just about to drive off to the dump, packed to the rafters with furniture and heavens knows what else. I fell back on some of my Irish charm to persuade the foreman fella to take the stuff to the storage depot till I had a chance to go through it, not that I've a clue whether it's even mine!'

'The will normally deals with those type of things,' the therapist said, unable to hold back a yawn. 'Not that I was privy to any of those private details. Ours was just a professional relationship,' the therapist stressed.

'Don't tell me you had old Morris sitting in the naughty chair talking about his misspent youth. That's bloody brilliant!'

'I simply responded to a call and assumed there was no one else available to help with the arrangements,' the therapist explained, remaining suitably vague.

'Well, it certainly wasn't going to be me, not having heard a peep out of the man for years.'

'So, you were in contact previously?'

'The last time he was invited over as a guest speaker at Dublin University.'

'And you were in attendance?'

'Not through choice. The newspaper thought it was worthy of coverage, being a famous name, plus the fact there was no one else available.'

'Which must have been extremely challenging.'

'Not especially. I just treated it as another assignment.'

'And there wasn't an opportunity to get closer during his visit?'

'Morris called the newspaper a good few times, but I wasn't interested. He'd made his bed – he could go ahead and lie in it as far as I was concerned!'

'How did your mother react to the news about Morris?' the therapist asked.

'It would have gone over her head. That's one good thing you can say about early dementia,' Jacob replied, showing a rare glimpse of emotion.

'Does she have any help?'

'If you call that Shay fella, she's been with him for the last ten years. He's probably donned that mantle he didn't sign up for.'

'And what changed your mind about coming now?'

There was a short pause while Jacob considered his response, then he answered, 'The last opportunity to find something positive about the person, who claimed to be my father.'

'An interesting perspective considering everything you say you went through.'

'I'd prefer to think of it as unfinished business,' Jacob said.

'In the meantime, you're welcome to have the spare room on the top floor and there's a bathroom at the end of the landing. You should be comfortable enough,' the therapist said, easing himself slowly up from his chair.

'Sounds good to me,' Jacob replied. A wee nightcap, first, wouldn't go amiss, wouldn't you agree?'

And before the therapist had a chance to respond, the same fellow began conducting an impromptu inspection of the room for any sign of alcohol.

'For the sake of our dear lord, don't tell me you're a teetotaller?' he exclaimed, soon becoming frustrated in his search.

'No, of course not,' the therapist hesitated, sitting down again. 'There's a drinks cupboard in the living room.'

'Grand!' Jacob exclaimed, taking the initiative to continue with his mission.

A few minutes later, he returned with a new bottle of Johnny Walker whisky and two crystal tumblers. Resuming his position at the table, he poured out two generous measures, handing one to his host.

'Cheers!' he toasted. 'To a new friendship,' and with that proceeded to down the beverage in a single gulp, leaving the other person looking horrified at the prospect of having to follow suit.

'Now, isn't that better for it?' Jacob said, topping up his tumbler with a further measure. 'It was clear enough I wasn't the person you'd expected, and twice in a day at that!'

'To be truthful, I wasn't sure I was able to provide the answers you were seeking,' the therapist replied, taking a small sip of his drink.

'That's as maybe but since fate seems to have thrown us together, I'll just have to make do.'

The other person laughed. Even if it was a back-handed compliment, it had lightened the atmosphere.

'Which makes me think it's a little strange I don't know a thing about *you*, wouldn't you say? I mean there are no photographs of your family here. You know none of the normal things you would expect,' Jacob noted, gazing at the bare walls. 'It looks as if you've covered up your past for some reason.'

'That's deliberate,' the therapist replied.

'Why's that then?' Jacob asked.

'I'm not normally at liberty to discuss anything about myself that's not directly related to patient's treatment.'

'But that doesn't make any sense! Applying those guidelines, assuming they'll fit the mould to whomever is sitting here, seems completely mad!'

'As long as I continue to treat people, I'm afraid that's how it has to be. It's a question of ethics. I'm sure you can understand.'

'And what about when you're not in your ivory tower? Surely, it can't be all work and no play, even for the likes of you, Simon?'

The absence of a response indicated the therapist was unwilling to be drawn.

'It just sems a bit ridiculous, that's all,' Jacob said, being the first to break the silence.

'I mean how can you expect to learn about yourself if you don't know how the person you've entrusted to help you, ticks?'

'But that's just the point, my professional position requires that I maintain the required level of objectivity, which would be impossible if I started talking about myself. Think of it as a judge knowing the plaintiff or the defendant. He would be obligated to excuse himself from the case.'

'Have it your way, but I just reckon you were running away, a bit like me!' Jacob concluded.

There was a lull in the conversation then,

'Going back to your father,' the therapist said, deftly changing tack.

'But why you?' Jacob interrupted. 'I mean there must have been a whole load of people he'd got close to during such an illustrious career.' The sarcasm was clear in his tone.

'I also wasn't his usual student. First, I was a good deal older and the fact I'd already a chosen career. Enrolling in his module was just to add another dimension,' the therapist explained.

'You mean you couldn't be influenced like the rest of them. From the little I know about the fella, that must have really got to him!'

'Perhaps, he rather looked on it as a challenge.'

'Appeared he met his match, is that right?'

'It certainly kept things interesting and provided plenty of stimulation,' the therapist replied.

'Brilliant! I can see it now, the rebel in the class.' Jacob gestured with an ark-like motion of his arms. 'You were his plant to keep the others on their toes. The problem with all of that is, it was the nature of the man to lose interest, once he'd achieved his purpose!' At which point he abruptly slammed his glass down on the table and got up to go. 'You won't mind if I avail myself of the contents of your bookshelves?'

'Do feel free. You know where to find them,' came the muffled response.

'You can tell a lot about a man from his choice of reading material,' Jacob said, giving a knowing look before he wandered off, leaving his host still seated and lightheaded from his second whisky of the evening.

3

The next morning, there was no sign of the overnight visitor. The only trace there had been anyone else in the house off the Golders Green Road were the two whisky tumblers and the half empty bottle on the kitchen table; that and gaps in the two bookshelves where a number of books had been withdrawn.

For a while, life went on like any other home that had taken in a lodger, Jacob appeared to be out for much of the day. By the time he came home his host was already fast asleep in bed quite content with the present arrangement and, cognisant of the fact the younger man was going through a period of complex personal adjustment, deciding it best to leave him to his own devices.

Then, a week later, the pattern suddenly changed when the front door to which Jacob had been provided with a spare key remained unlocked and the occupant failed to appear from his top floor room.

The reality was quite different. Jacob had wasted no time in claiming his inheritance and retrieved Morris's most private papers, hoping to find the will but instead discovering far more than he could have possibly anticipated.

A couple of days later, Jacob sensed someone outside on the landing.

'It's open, come in if you want,' he called out.

The therapist entered the room to find the occupant fully

dressed on the edge of the bed with his case packed. The contents of a large storage box were scattered haphazardly over the carpet. But it was a small stack of letters by his side accompanied by the distant expression that indicated he had suffered some sort of shock.

'I've not seen much of you and was just wanting to see if everything's all right,' the therapist enquired casually.

'It was a mistake, I should never have come,' Jacob lamented, giving no clue as to the reason for his distress.

'I assume something has occurred for you to regret that decision,' the therapist replied.

'I've got a ferry back to Cork at four pm, so I really should be getting going,' Jacob retorted, in no mood to go into detail. On reflection, it might have been better to knock the whole thing on the head and return home rather than face a new emotional upheaval. He'd got his life back together after a fashion. If he had any sense, he should have left it at that and moved on. However, it wasn't the first time his curiosity got the better of him and it probably wouldn't be the last, which is why he wasted no time pulling those papers out of storage in the first place.

'Did the letters contain bad news?' the therapist enquired.

'That depends on how you want to look at it. Let's just say it's completely thrown into turmoil everything I was led to believe.'

'And that's only just come to light?' the therapist asked.

'Seems Morris here was not quite the rascal he was reputed to be. Wouldn't you know it wasn't his decision to keep away?'

'Presumably, you've had time to think things through, so I wish you all the best and if I can be of any help, you know where to find me,' the therapist said, moving away.

'Wait, don't you want to talk about the letters?'

The therapist stopped and turned around.

'It was my mother. Look, they were returned unopened!' Jacob garbled thrusting the letters in the older man's direction. 'Morris pleaded with her to be allowed back into our lives, but it fell on deaf ears. Fair dos she wanted nothing to do with the fella, but she had no business denying me the right!'

'And what do you think you'll achieve going back to Ireland?' the therapist questioned.

'For goodness' sake, what was the woman thinking? It defies belief,' Jacob said, close to tears.

There was a short pause while he considered his options, then, 'What would I gain by staying?' he asked.

'It seems now you've learnt something you didn't know about your father, there may be other things as well that you'll discover,' the therapist observed glancing at the remainder of items that were, presumably, retrieved from the depot.

'And my mother, what do you suggest? Just forget all about it?'

'Jacob, it's quite natural to feel aggrieved but what would you achieve bringing up the subject, now she has dementia. Does she even know you're here?'

'You've got a point,' Jacob conceded. 'I suppose I've nothing to lose lingering a little longer, if you've got no other waif and stray waiting in line for the room, that is?'

'It's safe to say that can be put on hold for the time being,' the therapist retorted. Then, glancing at his watch, 'Right, a patient calls!' he exclaimed, hurrying away, this time without looking back.

'And just when you finished with the last one!' Jacob shouted after him before continuing his search through his father's possessions.

22

4

The change in atmosphere was as pronounced as much as it was immediate, typified none more so than by the disposition of the top-floor occupant. The dishevelled look matching his previously aggressive stance replaced by a calmer spruced up version, Jacob, now settled in his surroundings, admitted this was was solely due to the staid older man he'd come across purely by chance. That their discussions merely provided a sounding board to vent his frustration at the difficulties he was forced to endure, he now appreciated were just a passive attempt by his host to bolster a diminished sense of self-worth of which, he, Jacob was blissfully unaware.

The momentum of self-discovery that had begun with the letters to his mother continued, as predicted, with the press cuttings of his reports which had afforded his father sole opportunity to form a profile of a child who was destined to remain at a distance. How ironic that <u>he</u> was now involved in the same process in the reverse with the added input of his mentor's valuable first-hand experience.

Establishing the Barnets derived from Germany and had exchanged the decadent Berlin of the 1920's for the more salubrious white shores of Dover, gave him rare insight into the family from which he derived but sadly had never got to know. But it was the photographic albums kept in pristine condition and seeing his uncanny likeness particularly to members of the male line into which he unconsciously morphed so that paternity couldn't be denied.

Jacob was in a reflective mood at his usual table in the station café, now deplete of its morning trade, with only his newspaper for company. Realising he was practically out of money, plus the fact of knowing he couldn't take advantage of the same hospitality indefinitely, he needed to find ways of supporting himself again. So much had occurred over the last few weeks, making it difficult to establish what life had next in store. The prospect of a return to Ireland, which he had only put off at the last moment, had lost much of its appeal and with it, his one source of income. His mother was still taboo as far as he was concerned and even his long-standing girlfriend, Kayleigh, whose prediction that their break may end up being permanent, couldn't really claim surprise if it were to prove accurate. The truth was the closeness he felt to his father in death of which he was deprived during his lifetime, enabled him to look on this hitherto unknown part of northwest London as his real home.

Flipping aimlessly through the paper, he stopped abruptly when he reached the Obituary page. In common with the previous additions, it suddenly occurred to him there hadn't been anything to date on the much-acclaimed Morris Barnet, which, considering the high esteemed manner in which he was held in the academic world over the past three decades, seemed remiss in the extreme. Jacob now felt a strong urge to put that right.

Fortunately, he'd already accessed a large quantity of his father's work from storage, so he wouldn't exactly be starting from scratch.

Jacob found the therapist at work when he returned late one evening not long after.

'Burning the midnight oil again, I see,' he said, dropping a clear plastic folder on his desk.

The therapist stopped what he was doing and cast his eye over the piece submitted to the main Fleet Street papers.

'Thought you might be interested,' he added, noticing the immediate reaction it had caused.

'What type of response do you expect?' the therapist asked.

'The boys at home would jump on it. Over here, I had to pay up front for the insertion before they even gave me the time of day!'

'So, there's no guarantee it'll be printed?'

Jacob produced a wry smile, indicating that he'd left nothing to chance.

'That's why I've kept this little snippet here in reserve,' he revealed, holding up a piece entitled *Discovering My Father* by Jacob Barnet.

'Quite a ploy,' the older man enthused.

'Just enough to whet their appetite, wouldn't you say?'

'I assume there's more where that came from?'

'How do you think I've been spending my time these last weeks in that top floor room of yours, apart from reading you out of house and home, that is?'

'I'd imagine you'll have them bidding against each other for the rights,' the therapist said.

'Got to get back on my feet,' somehow Jacob came back, 'which reminds me, it's time for me to start looking for alternative accommodation.'

'Yes, of course, whatever you think best, but there's no hurry from my point of view,' the therapist replied.

'It's just that I've grown a little too comfortable here, which won't best prepare me for the challenges that lie ahead,' Jacob stressed.

'And how about Ireland?' the therapist queried.

'That was a previous life, which is now best behind me,' Jacob said with sparse regret. He didn't bother mentioning that he had already laid the foundations for this eventuality weeks earlier. The fact he managed to pay off his share of the rent on the one bed flat on the Dublin Road and then lean on his friend, Eamon Dunne, at the paper to organise the shipment of the rest of his things, was testimony to the flimsiness of his roots to the place, or so he'd convinced himself.

'Right, what are your plans for the rest of the evening?' Jacob asked.

'I've got some work to finish off for tomorrow and then…'

'Get your coat on, we're going out, my treat,' Jacob interrupted.

'To a restaurant?' the therapist enquired, incredulously.

'A burger and chips on the Regent's canal is hardly a celebration for a whole new beginning; surely Simon, even you can see that?'

5

Early the next morning, there was a sound of voices outside in the road belonging to a sizeable gathering of reporters, trying to the attract the attention of a well-prepared Jacob Barnet with a barrage of questions.

'When did you discover Morris Barnet was your father?' a scruffy male yelled.

'Tell us how he managed to keep it under wraps for so many years,' his partner in arms followed up.

'All will be revealed in good time,' Jacob replied. 'Thanks for coming and, as they say in your line of business, watch this space.'

Jacob remained unfazed. After all, how many times had he been standing in the same position desperate for a story so they wouldn't have to go back to their editors empty-handed?

The disgruntled throng, realising their worst-case scenario was about to be realised, began to disperse, when a young female journalist stepped forward.

'Jane French, *Sunday Times*,' she said, introducing herself. 'Jacob, can we assume *Discovering My Father* is just a taster of things to come?' she asked, making specific reference to the extract accompanying the insert.

'Well, it's a bit too early to talk about that,' he replied, caught off guard.

'When you do want to talk about it, feel free to contact me,' she added, offering her calling card.

Jacob instinctively went up and took the details and returned to the house, gauging how long it would be before he made the call and confident the insert of Morris Barnet's obituary was now a foregone conclusion.

*

An emergency meeting of the academic council was underway to consider the bombshell that hit the university that morning. A glum-faced vice chancellor together with with six heads of faculty sat around the boardroom table, the photograph of the late Morris Barnet peering ominously out at them from the editions of all the main newspapers, while waiting anxiously for the opinion from legal services. Had it been just for the belated appearance of the obituaries, it might not have generated such concern, albeit the intransigence it displayed supplying the same newspapers with its list of the controversial figure's achievements was not without risk of sooner or later being exposed by a former student. The problem was the sudden appearance of the son and his apparent pursuit of the recognition due to his father. That the main body of Barnet's work, produced when he was still employed, belonged to the university was irrefutable but it was the last and potentially the most important part he was working on when he died which was now precariously at stake.

*

Less than a week later, Jacob entered the London Bridge offices of the *The Times*. He gave his name to reception, pinned his visitor's badge onto the lapel of his leather bomber jacket and, as instructed, took the lift to the second floor.

The reaction to his piece on his father was uniform in its exuberance from every newspaper clamouring for an exclusive on his relationship with the hitherto forgotten philosopher. The fact that Morris Barnet managed to influence generations of young people for then to leave no trace of his accomplishments, just because he'd disappeared from view, now seemed even more mysterious.

The same female reporter was there when he arrived.

'Jacob, it's good to see you again,' she said, extending her arm to him. 'Please follow me,' and began striding ahead through an open plan office, already a hive of activity at eight-thirty in the morning.

'You didn't exactly give me much choice,' Jacob quipped, trying to keep up and thinking how the state-of-the-art pressroom had little in common with the antiquated printshop that served his local Irish community.

'I'd be surprised if we are the only interested party,' she said,

A minute later, they entered the editor's glass enclosure.

'Damien, this is Jacob Barnet,' the reporter announced, endeavouring to draw the attention of a cropped-haired individual pouring over the latest newspaper copy that had just landed on his desk.

'Be with you in a second,' the editor said, giving the piece a final look over.

'Right, that caught us a bit by surprise,' he added, whilst giving the thumbs up to a passing colleague, indicating the copy was good to go.

'And, why's that?' Jacob replied, taking an instant dislike to the fellow leaning back in his chair.

'For a start, we didn't know much about this esteemed

professor of yours until his obituary suddenly appeared courtesy of his apparently long-lost son.'

'Doesn't say much for your organisation then, when possibly one of the foremost academics in his field escapes the interest of what purports to be the capital's most established newspaper,' Jacob retorted, beginning to wonder why he'd bothered coming.

'I didn't mean it was not of interest,' the editor retracted, suspecting he may have overstepped the mark. 'But looking at it from our point of view, the first thing we did, or should I say tried to do, was to authenticate your story. You can appreciate that any paper worth its salt wouldn't take something as sensational as this at face value.'

There was a short pause while Jacob considered his response. On reflection, what the man said made complete sense. In truth, he hadn't expected it to have gone this far. Limited coverage of the person's life that obviously meant more to him than anyone else, was probably all he could have reasonably hoped for, unless there was something in addition, they weren't telling him.

'What did you mean by sensational?' he probed.

'The fact the university he taught at gave us the cold shoulder when we asked for its take on their former lecturer!'

'When was that exactly?' Jacob asked. There hadn't been sufficient time to make those enquiries before they went to press, he pondered. The only explanation was that they must have known about his father's death beforehand.

'A rookie reporter of ours, Lucien, who's got a good nose for a good story, sees a bit of kerfuffle in one of those quaint streets up in Hampstead. He makes a few enquiries what its all about and comes away with a spin on a celebrity in the area who's just popped his clogs and how the local property sharks were trying to get their hands on his former home. It's not exactly novel, but we wanted to give the lad a chance, so we decided to take it further.'

'But that makes no sense,' Jacob said, now seeing the real reason for their keenness.

'The chaps on the other papers got the same response, surprisingly there are occasions when we share information, or in this case, the lack of it,' the editor continued.

'So, when we received your blurb, we decided to go with it instead,' the female reporter said, speaking for the first time. 'After all, it was a much better story, which is why we'd be open to the possibility of serialising it.'

'And the university?' Jacob asked, seemingly oblivious to the proposal.

'No longer of interest,' the editor intervened. 'Anyway, you'd be better off pursuing them yourself if you think they're hiding something.'

'Conveniently passing the buck, it seems to me,' Jacob quipped.

The man's smirk said it all. Why utilise valuable resources on an uncertain project when there was a decent story ready to go that didn't carry the risk of getting sued?

'So, where do we go from here?' Jacob asked impatiently.

'I think it's fair to say there's a modicum of interest on our part, assuming there's more where this came from.' He gestured to the extract he mentioned.

Jacob recognised the tactic of indifference. Don't show your hand so as not to weaken your negotiating stance. The reality was the paper of its repute wouldn't have given him the time of day if it wasn't seriously interested. It was tempting to call its bluff.

'That shouldn't be a problem,' he replied.

'You've got ten days, should be more than enough time to come up with a half decent six-parter,' the editor said finally, then carried on with the rest of his morning's work.

Jacob, feeling he'd just been dismissed after being up against the form teacher at his primary school, was keen to get away, when Jane French caught up with him.

'Are you pleased?' she said, grinning broadly. 'You should be.'

'Not quite what I'd expected,' he replied, carrying on his way out of the building.

'I don't think you quite realise what's on offer here,' she called after him.

But it fell on deaf ears. Jacob, at least in his mind, was already back at his sanctuary in northwest London.

*

Jacob took up his now familiar position in the first-floor consulting room. The truth was the meeting at *The Times* had left him feeling unsettled, which is why he needed to recount his experience.

'Haven't you considered the possibility you're being too harsh on yourself?' the therapist mooted. 'From what you implied previously, you'd happily have settled for what the paper is offering you.'

'That's the whole point. It wasn't supposed to be about me!' Jacob retorted. 'My father is the priority here. Surely, you can see that?'

'So, you're feeling that you'd be exploiting his name in some way?'

'That's exactly right!'

'Jacob, look on it as a journey. You've come a long way, first coming to terms with your past, ridding yourself of the negative sentiments with which you were consumed. Then, finding a positive path, which in your case involved forging a posthumous relationship with your father, but that's only the first stage.'

'And, what's the next one about exactly?'

'You, Jacob.'

'But that's whom I thought I needed to get away from?'

'You're right. But you've seen yourself you're not that person sat in that chair three months ago.'

'I wasn't aware you were keeping note. Is this some gentle way of landing me with a bill for time spent by any chance?' Jacob quipped.

'No, not at all.' The therapist smiled. 'Although, a good word in my direction wouldn't go amiss,' he came back with uncharacteristic levity.

'My goodness, I wouldn't have put you down as one touting for business!'

'Just a bit of self-preservation, which sometimes gets forgotten, especially with altruistic pursuits,' the therapist clarified.

'Mine or yours?' Jacob jested.

The therapist offered no response.

'Survival in this cruel world of ours, and as if I of all people needed reminding!'

'And it's not like you'd be starting from scratch,' the therapist added.

'You mean as a writer?' Jacob replied pensively.

'You seem to have convinced everyone other than yourself where your talent lies. Remember, things rarely happen on their own, if you don't take the first step.'

Jacob thought for a moment. Realising he'd merely been presented with an analogy of his own predicament, it was up to him to find the way forward. There was no denying he'd tried running before he could walk. Now to stop him falling flat on his face, he needed to start using his head, having gained the clarity that was missing.

'So, I'll go ahead with the serialisation, provided the supplement comes up with a fair wage, and take it from there. That's what I'll do,' Jacob said, feeling more confident about his future.

6

For the next week, Jacob took himself to the British Library at Euston. The imposed silence suited a newly discovered sense of self-discipline. Rarely lifting his head from his old laptop and oblivious to the concerned looks from all around, he single-mindedly set about his task putting down on screen the troubled childhood. Then, growing up in Ireland, devoid of a guiding influence and only an uncertain future ahead, never envisaging the dramatic change in his life brought about by the belated discovery of his father, nothing was omitted.

When he finished a day early, he spent time going through and checking every word and nuance. Suddenly, the thought struck him there was so much more that needed to be said. In the main, there was next to nothing on the university where his father taught for thirty years and from whom, curiously, there was still no reaction to his obituary. The choice was either to pay them a visit in the time he had left or submit the piece as is and hope for the best. Recalling the need to start making ends meet, it didn't take long to decide on the latter.

For the next week, Jacob waited with bated breath for a response from the paper. All six articles were delivered personally by hand. Now there was nothing more he could do but wait. More seriously, he was completely out of money and even contemplated going cap in hand to the few Irish relations with whom he was still on speaking terms.

One spring afternoon, on a particular long walk that routinely helped to clear his head, Jacob found himself in the pretty lane within a stone's throw of Hampstead Heath where his father had lived. Assuming there must be new people living there or that the property was still undergoing refurbishment, he was astonished to find the white-stucco villa in exactly the same state as four months earlier without any sign of life. Suddenly, he recognised one of the young male estate agents striding down the street.

'Wouldn't waste your time looking at that, if I were you,' he said from a short distance away. 'There are far easier ways of making a living!' and carried on resolutely to his next appointment.

Jacob could only assume the transaction had fallen through for some reason and that there wasn't subsequent interest. Except the hint of something untoward led him to think that it might just be worth pursuing.

He was just about to wend his way home, when he received a terse email on his mobile phone from a legal firm requesting his presence at their offices at the earliest opportunity.

7

The next day, Jacob entered the Marylebone Offices of Robson Charles solicitors. The fact that the previous vengeful disposition against his father, which would have pushed for the meeting earlier, was replaced with a sense of foreboding for gaining unauthorised access to his private items from storage, was testimony that he'd moved on but didn't offer much comfort.

Providing his name to a bored-looking young chap manning the reception, Jacob was directed to take the lift to the meeting room on the third floor of the ornate Grade II listed building.

He entered a bright space with a direct view over west London, and seated at a large boardroom table was an elderly flush-faced man, trussed up in a double-breasted suit that was so tight that it appeared in danger of cutting off his oxygen supply, next to whom was an alert male assistant to provide support if called upon.

'You must be Jacob,' the senior lawyer croaked, deigning to acknowledge his visitor. 'It's opportune to meet you at last.'

'Oh, and why might that be?' Jacob replied, taking a seat at the opposite end.

'Firstly, allow me to express my condolences regarding the loss of your father,' the lawyer said with a false show of sympathy.

'That's very kind. How long did you represent his

interests?' Jacob enquired.

'Whilst I never had any dealings personally, the firm's connection goes back a good number of years,' the same person hedged. 'Still, that's now bye the bye. We're here to go through the last will and testament of the late Morris Barnet.' He glanced at the official document in front of him.

'I was aware he left one,' Jacob said, relieved that his initial fears appeared unfounded.

'Very much so. I'm at liberty to inform you, as the sole beneficiary, you stand to inherit the estate.'

'That would make a change, being on the receiving end of good fortune for once,' he added lightly.

'Yes, quite so, although I have to say, there may not be quite the amount you might have expected, at least to start off with,' the stuffy fellow clarified. 'James, how much is there standing in the bank account?' he said, turning to the young man on his left.

'Just over three hundred thousand pounds at the close,' the junior solicitor replied.

Jacob was aghast! These were just telephone numbers in his world!

'I doubt the personal effects would add up to much considering the current state of the property,' his superior sneered.

'Surely, that would be for me to decide. After all, you already informed me I'm the only beneficiary. Isn't that, right?' Jacob said, unsure whether he'd heard correctly.

'Yes, quite so, which is why the meeting couldn't have come at a more opportune time,' Robson blustered.

Jacob sensed there was something which the old fella was holding back and was curious to find out what it was.

'So, whatever little value those particular items hold, I assume it's down to me to do with them as I see fit?'

'And the proceeds of the bank account, once the authorisation is given to put it in your name,' the younger brief added, attracting an angry look from the solicitor that his junior had overstepped the mark.

'So, my question is what was the reason for the delay?' Jacob asked, sensing he might be gaining the upper hand.

'Negotiations with the Revenue are rarely straight forward. Then, granting probate is frequently a lengthy process,' the solicitor waffled.

'Which I assume, now concluded, I can take possession of my inheritance. But what I fail to understand is why all of this couldn't have been laid out in an email? It would have saved a lot of time, unless there's possibly another reason I don't know about,' Jacob said, trying to draw the fellow out.

Just then, the solicitor checked his pocket watch.

'You must excuse me, I've got another meeting starting in a few minutes. James will run through the outstanding points,' he said, eager to get away before disappearing quickly from view.

Jacob looked on while the young solicitor followed his superior's exit with a raise of his eyebrows.

'Good to know this isn't the most important thing on his agenda,' Jacob said mockingly.

'I wouldn't presume that. However, the truth is the firm has rather found itself with egg on its face at this time,' the junior lawyer divulged.

'And what's that got to do with me?'

'Quite a lot, actually. Let me explain.'

Jacob waited with bated breath while the other person

referred to his notes.

'It concerns the property in Hampstead.'

'The house occupied by my father,' Jacob clarified.

'Yes, but it has recently come to light that it goes a bit further than that.'

'You've lost me,' Jacob replied, baffled as to what might be forthcoming.

'Briefly, the property, contrary to what was believed, maybe part of the estate.'

'You mean my father was the owner after all?'

'So, it appears from the documentation.'

'And how can it be you just happened to have found out about it?' Jacob queried. Clearly, something didn't make sense. Whether there was anything underhand or some simple mistake was hard to predict.

'Seems the previous firm failed to register the title with the Land Registry.'

Jacob didn't need to second guess who was responsible, which probably accounted for old Robson's keenness to duck the issue a few minutes earlier.

'I'm still not sure what you are saying.'

'Once we've submitted the corrected documentation, so long as we can show uninterrupted use, there's no reason why the property shouldn't revert to you. The question is whether sufficient evidence exists and whether you might be able to lay your hands on it.'

Jacob pondered on the dilemma. Now he realised why there had been no movement on the property for the past months. With no proof of ownership, there was no option but to leave the place vacant to deteriorate further, which explained the estate agent's caustic comment having found himself deprived of a lucrative commission on the sale.

'So, unless I can come up with goods, I lose my inheritance, and you fellas, whose fault it is, merely brush your hands and walk away. That doesn't sound right. Surely, you can see that?' Jacob didn't disclose he'd already got all the proof he needed from his father's records.

'I can sympathise with your predicament but from time-to-time things do get overlooked. Of course, you're at liberty to register a complaint with the law society but considering how much time has elapsed, it's unlikely to succeed.'

'Sounds like I'm on a hiding to nothing,' Jacob replied.

'My suggestion, for what its worth, would be to prioritise obtaining proof of continuous occupation. Time is of the essence because, as a *bona vacantia*, ownerless property reverts to the crown.'

'I suppose that's one way of guaranteeing the Royals are never short of a quid or two!' Jacob quipped, getting to his feet.

'You've got a point,' the young lawyer replied, gathering up his papers. 'Here's your copy of the will, which you should have received.'

'Just another unintentional mishap?' Jacob said, the sarcasm clear in his tone. Taking the document he'd had sight of for the first time, he left the building with only one thing on his mind, not taking possession of his inheritance but instead a feeling of profound sadness that Morris Barnet couldn't have done more to establish a paternal relationship and that he, Jacob, had played a significant part in denying his father the opportunity.

8

Four weeks later, Jacob moved unnoticed into his father's house at 31 Willow Row.

With none of the usual rustling of curtains that accompanied even the slightest deviation he'd come to believe as the norm, it was if he'd already become persona non grata with his neighbours without having met a single one of them. Then, he had to remind himself this wasn't Shandon Street, Cork, but an affluent patch within a few miles of central London. His initial reticence dispelled by the man to whom he owed so much, Jacob now appreciated what the therapist had meant about taking control of his own life. Not that it didn't come with a whole set of new responsibilities from which, up till now, he would gladly have shied away.

Foremost, was how to support a lifestyle devoid of any prospects of making a decent living. The difference was that it was his decision and his alone to take on the property. Fortunately, the money in the bank was still largely intact even after a sizeable amount of inheritance tax paid to the Revenue as a result of putting the property in his name.

One morning shortly after, when he was halfway up a ladder attending to a blocked gutter, there was the sound of footsteps coming down the garden path. Looking down, he spotted the diminutive figure of Jane French from *The Times*, standing there.

'Hang on for a few minutes, will you? I've got my hands dirty right now,' he shouted down, in no particular hurry to finish the task. With everything else going on over the past few weeks, he hadn't given more than a passing thought to the female journalist or her publication.

'So, to what do I owe this pleasure?' Jacob enquired, heading back into the house. With a lack of any form of response from her paper, he'd assumed it had lost interest.

'I thought I'd drop by since I was in the area,' the journalist explained, following closely behind.

'That's a little surprising since I hadn't heard back from you.'

'It's not what you might imagine,' she said, stepping into the spacious entrance hall.

'You mean other than that editor of yours identifying an even cheaper story to get his hands on!'

'I wouldn't know what Damien's up to since I'm not at the paper anymore,' the young woman divulged. 'Though, it looks like you've landed on your feet with this place,' she said, busily taking in her impressive surroundings.

'Don't tell me, the man put the boot in?' Jacob quizzed.

'Let's just say we didn't see eye to eye on a number of different issues.'

'So, how did you manage to track me down, or is that a daft question?' Jacob probed, expecting there was more to it.

'More luck than judgment actually, that was until I recalled it was Lucien who'd initially drawn our attention to the place. Anyway, he wasn't too pleased that he was taken off the story.'

'I know how he feels,' Jacob interjected.

'So, he used his initiative to continue doing a bit of

digging around, asking a few questions at the university; you know that sort of thing. But as soon as he mentions your name, finding the door slammed in his face, he realised he'd hit a nerve.'

'Probably, when they caught sight of the obituary,' Jacob surmised. 'Although, why it should have had that effect, does seem odd.'

'Unless there was something else going on?' Jane posed.

'Even so, it doesn't explain where I'd fit into the picture. I suppose it'll all come out in the wash one day,' Jacob replied, giving the impression he wasn't taking it too seriously.

'But that's not all,' the young woman went on, determined to have her say.

'Just as Lucien was leaving, there were those disparaging remarks he overheard from two senior members of the faculty over some belated work to do with Morris Barnet. It was as if it had resulted in him being discredited in some way. For what it's worth, my instinct tells me there's something big going down at CLU.'

'You're suggesting they're hiding it for some reason?'

'And they're terrified at being exposed, which was why, when you didn't respond to my calls, I decided to take a chance to come here in person.'

Jacob shrugged, not bothering to disclose his phone was on the blink and that he hadn't got around to replacing it.

'Thanks for the lowdown, but would I be right in thinking there's a bit more to your visit than just out of the goodness of your heart?'

'Jacob, my intuition tells me there's a story here.'

'As was the case with the serialisation, if I remember correctly?'

'Forget the supplement. They had their chance. And there are always other outlets. All I'm saying is that it could well be opportune they blew it because most of the stuff will be fresh to use on something else.'

'What do you have in mind?' Jacob asked with more interest.

'A factual or semi factual account of your experience, discovering your father, that type of thing. Spiced up a bit with getting to the bottom of what the university's up to wouldn't do its chances any harm,' she added casually. 'Oh, and it might be prudent having some friendly legal advice in the wings. These things can get a bit messy! Anyway, do give it some thought. I'm in between jobs right now but you can always get hold of me on this,' she said, texting her number before making her way back out through the open door.

9

Over the next few days, Jacob struggled to give some semblance of order to what appeared up till now to be two unreconcilable priorities. On the one hand, he was desperate to start generating a regular income unless he was going to find himself out on the street, making him think more than once he'd been too hasty in taking on a property, already threatening to soak up more money than he could get his hands on. And yet, he felt burdened with an obligation to restore the home bequeathed to him. More seriously, with everything else taking precedence, he'd side-stepped the long overdue accolade to his father. Suddenly, he recalled the therapist's analogy concerning self-preservation. Far from feeling compromised, he needed to be reminded that, in the real world, providing for himself first had to be the order of things. Almost immediately, Jacob felt a weight lifted from his shoulders. Now, he could freely apply his mind to both objectives.

The makeshift office that had previously housed his father's study, newly furnished with the works of Oscar Wilde and Bernard Shaw that had been shipped over from Ireland with rest of his belongings, were indicative the place had taken on a degree of permanence.

Reconsidering he shouldn't give up on the prospect of serialisation, Jacob considered contacting other publications that had printed the obituary. After all, the work was all ready to go. It seemed a waste of the time he'd spent at the British library for it not to be taken advantage of, plus the fact it would provide some much-needed short-term capital.

Recalling what Jane French had mentioned about the incident at the university, he began a search through his father's papers, hoping that it might throw some light on the issue.

Coming up with nothing, he remembered what appeared to be a wall safe, partially covered by a thick curtain. Gaining access was another matter, so it was easier putting it out of his mind. Now, he saw there was a small key on the bunch given to him by the solicitors, which had obviously escaped his notice.

Taking a chance, he went over and tried the lock. He wasn't disappointed. The door sprung open. Empty, apart from a thick brown envelope, Jacob ripped open the seal to find a manuscript. His initial thought was that it was just a piece of research locked away for safe keeping, except it seemed an extreme step when the remainder of his father's work was in the public domain, unless the intention was to withhold it for some reason.

Putting aside his plans for the rest of the day, Jacob settled down with only the document for company, seeing if he could throw some light on the subject.

Delving into it further, however, it soon appeared there was something distinctly suspicious about the piece. Firstly, the theme of *accommodating a higher force* led him to deduce it was either authored by someone else or as a result of a serious mental aberration on Morris Barnet's part. Either way, he needed to know whether it could be taken seriously.

Jacob sat waiting for the man ensconced behind his desk to comment on the hundred-page manuscript he'd only had sight of forty-eight hours earlier.

'You mentioned you're concerned about its authenticity,' the therapist remarked, putting the script back together.

'Well, it's a bit of a deviation from his usual stance, wouldn't you say?' Jacob replied. 'I mean for a fella spending his whole life in denial of the existence of anyone or anything outside his so called-called superior level of understanding to then suddenly claim that he might have got it all wrong, sounds a bit like hedging his bets at the last moment.'

'It's not uncommon for people in their later stages of life to seek comfort in something they may have previously discounted as irrelevant or unimportant. Look at it, if you will, as recognition of their own mortality,' the therapist explained.

'You mean the arrogance of youth can no longer be relied upon to hold them in good stead.'

'There is an aspect of acceptance to it.'

'And you think that was a likely scenario with Morris?' Jacob queried, finding it all too unrealistic.

'It's interesting that you regard it as a suggestion of weakness on his part.'

'Well, if it isn't, it'd be a hell of a climb down,' Jacob retorted.

'To be open to the possibility of there being a greater force at play doesn't necessarily contradict his theory of man influencing his own destiny,' the therapist countered.

'Then, I've obviously missed something.' The truth was

it had completely gone against the image he'd built up about the father he'd only recently got to know. Now he was being asked to accept a completely different version, he'd felt he'd gone right back to square one.

'Perhaps, it would be easier trying to relate it to your own experience,' the therapist continued.

'Back to <u>my</u> journey of self-discovery, is that it?' Jacob replied, feeling unsettled.

'There are certain similarities. Admittedly, your father wasn't forced to contend with the same disadvantages in early life.'

'I remember, born into a life of privilege, never knowing what it's like to go without. Is that the type of thing you mean?' A trace of the former resentment evident in his tone.

'More in terms of being imbued with a strong sense of identity, whereas you were having to find it for yourself.'

'I still don't see the parallel,' Jacob said.

'That's because Morris jumped a couple of more steps. With a career laid out for him and a supportive background, as you discovered, success wasn't slow in forthcoming.'

'You're saying he took it for granted.'

'He probably didn't know any different.'

'Sounds like we had even less in common than I'd assumed!'

'The problem was it didn't adequately prepare him to deal with misfortune when it struck.'

'He should have come and asked me, then,' Jacob said, half-heartedly.

There was a short pause, then the therapist continued.

'For example, have you considered the effect that last unanswered letter might have had on your father?

Consider for a moment the impact of being thwarted from having contact with his only flesh and blood.'

'You mean, when he knew his time was up?' Jacob said.

'By then, it was probably too late,' the therapist replied.

'The final act of a desperate man,' Jacob muttered, shaking his head sadly.

There was another short pause.

'But the influence he apparently had on so many young peoples' lives, you said as much in your address, must have presumably counted for something?' Jacob said, the first to break the silence.

'It may have compensated to some extent, but it doesn't make up for a parent being unable to pass the same on to their only child.'

Jacob became pensive. In all of this, he'd only ever focused on himself as the damaged party and failed to see the other side.

'I hadn't considered that before,' he admitted.

'Whether he realised it or not, and these things are often subconscious, your father probably felt vulnerable for the first time in his life.'

'In other words, he didn't have the answers to his own dilemma… and that would have been sufficient to turn his life's work on its head?… that seems a bit far-fetched!'

'It might have been just enough to sow a seed of doubt. The salient point is that he felt the need to share that uncertainty with his public,' the therapist replied.

'You're implying that he couldn't very well leave this world having led it up the garden path.'

'There may have been an element of atonement he'd been witnessing.'

'Nothing like a good talking to in a confession box.

Those priests would have had a field day at old Morris's expense, wouldn't you say?'

'You still seem to view it as a retraction, but it might just as well be regarded as a final stage in the process.'

'I'm not with you.'

'Just because Morris had encountered some un-resolvable problems in life, it doesn't have to detract from his earlier achievements. In fact, it could be that it laid the foundations for his most important work.'

'You mean his *Magnum Opus.* So, that's what this last message is all about, is it? Not having all the answers?'

'Some of the greatest early thinkers attributed the highest form of wisdom to that very thing.'

'But doesn't that presuppose there's someone else that does?'

'For those of faith that certainly is the case.'

'Belief in the so called merciful one who permits the innocent to suffer while the wicked get away scot-free, is that who you mean?'

'Some might choose to view it that way.'

'What other way is there?'

'Emerging from a hardship from which there appeared no hope, for example?'

'That doesn't begin to answer the question,' Jacob retorted.

'Maybe so, but it's possibly the closest one's going to get. Alternatively, ask yourself whether it's reasonable to use what appears to us as a gross injustice to others, of which we have no real understanding, let alone control, to detract from a personal experience that, conversely, might have been just as positive?'

There was a pause while Jacob reflected on his own

predicament and how, if he were completely honest, he could never have envisaged the dramatic turn of events in such a short period of time.

'That still seems a roundabout way to go about things, when you could have quite as easily skipped the first part!' he countered.

'But that's the point. Those same teachings are all about learning to deal with the initial phase,' the therapist replied.

'And the rest takes care of itself, is that it?'

'Eventually, but it can be a lengthy process. Taking responsibility for one's own life, is rarely straightforward, especially if there's a genuine grievance early on.'

'Tell me about it! I wrote the book,' Jacob shrugged, not at all sure he went along with it all. Then, he had another thought. 'Surely, you're not telling me Morris here would have been exposed to those type of teachings?'

'You're doubtful because he'd previously ruled out such things,' the therapist replied.

'It just doesn't fit the profile of the fella,' Jacob protested. Suddenly, he recalled the family photo he'd recovered from storage and remembered being taken aback by the strange garb of a bearded man in a black frock coat and crocheted head covering, who seemed totally out of keeping with the rest, now wondering if there was any possible connection.

'Conceivably, that might have made it more likely for him to be influenced by them,' the therapist said, placing a deferential hand on a collection of old writings that appeared by his side.

Jacob, instinctively, homed in on a display cabinet filled with similar leather-bound volumes, which assuming were the exclusive domain of its owner, he'd purposely given a wide berth.

'I wouldn't have minded being a fly on a wall while all this was going on,' Jacob divulged.

'You're referring to your father's thought process and whether it was likely to have been a smooth transition?'

'Well, he'd be taking a hell of a chance of being discredited, wouldn't you say? On the other hand, maybe only a man like Morris could get away with it! It's just a shame he was denied the opportunity of expounding his thoughts in person,' Jacob concluded.

'Even more reason to leave it up to the reader to draw his or her own conclusions,' the therapist added.

'And that's what you're suggesting I should do, is it?'

There was no response but also no misinterpreting the therapist's knowing look.

*

Jacob made his way back to Hampstead, his head buzzing with the latest revelation about Morris Barnet, the father it was clear he still hadn't fully got to know. Ironically, although their trajectories couldn't have been more diverse, the adversity they shared brought them together in the most unimaginable way. Strangely, the emotional upheaval that had only come to the fore later in an otherwise charmed life may have been a harder adjustment for his father than his own troubled experience of never knowing anything different. Even latterly, when he learnt otherwise, it was more about finding out who Morris Barnet really was rather than carving out an identity for himself.

Slowly, everything began to fall into place. The heated exchange between the dons was presumably over his father's posthumous work, adding credence to the possibility of some underhand dealings by the university.

The question was what they were hiding and why? The next step was to find out for himself what was going on.

10

Two days later, Jacob strode up the steps of the 19th century neo-classical building off Bloomsbury square. Bypassing an unmanned reception, he headed to the philosophy faculty, which, he'd established, constituted a couple of rooms on the first floor. Dispensing with the need to go through the normal channels, he resorted, instead, to the well-tested tactic of the element of surprise that had served him in good stead in the past. After all, it wasn't as if he wasn't fully equipped, now the recently discovered manuscript had been accredited, at least in his own mind, to Morris Barnet's long awaited *Magnum Opus*, it provided him with the best possible credentials to ensure its author received his rightful acclaim.

A few minutes later, confronted in the corridor by a group of undergraduates leaving the department, Jacob nonchalantly passed the through the open door. Without acknowledging the thin man in a robe and mortarboard collating the notes from his lecture, Jacob began an impromptu inspection of what was once his father's exclusive domain, when the Dean, sensing he wasn't alone, called out,

'Forgotten something?'

'You'd be better asking yourself that!' Jacob replied, carrying on looking for any remnants of the former professor's influence.

'Excuse me, and who are you exactly?'

'Jacob Barnet. You're no doubt familiar with the name?'

The man, seeming if he'd been struck by lightning, was unable to muster a response.

'Surely, you can't have forgotten the emeritus professor of philosophy, author of thirty-eight essays on the power of the individual and numerous other works. Come on, he helped put this place of yours on the map!'

'No, of course not. Indeed, a most valued member of staff,' the Dean replied, staging a remarkable recovery.

'Which makes the whole way he was treated even more bizarre. I mean the deathly silence by the university on Morris Barnet. As you said, he wasn't your ordinary run of the mill type of fella.'

'Quite so, he made an invaluable contribution to the faculty.'

'And yet, you deemed it unworthy of any acclaim whatsoever. In fact, I'd wager you went out of your way to ensure the man didn't get what was due to him… Why was that?' Jacob probed.

'Mr Barnet, that's a serious allegation and quite without any foundation!' The Dean retorted defensively. He'd become flushed in the face and, despite the cool temperature in the room, had begun to perspire.

'In that case, perhaps you can explain the absence of any obituary when he died?' Jacob purposely didn't mention the blank treatment handed out to the young journalist he'd heard about, when the chap brought up the subject.

'There are a number of issues that recently came to light of which you'll probably unaware,' the Dean said.

'I'd certainly be interested to know what they are but don't see how they could have had any impact on such an esteemed career,' Jacob replied.

'No one here is suggesting otherwise. We're naturally appreciative of the contribution Morris Barnet made but I'm afraid, in recent years, he'd rather lost his way.'

'You're saying his face no longer fitted for some reason,' Jacob retorted taken aback by the inference of a dismissal.

'Let's just say, we didn't see eye to eye on certain changes to the module he'd proposed to implement.'

Jacob didn't need it spelling out the Dean was referring to the controversial stance of his father's last work.

'And that was sufficient reason to give the man the boot, was it?'

'We'd prefer to term it as early retirement. Morris hadn't enjoyed the most robust of health. I can assure you, it was an arrangement which suited both parties.'

Jacob could only imagine the anguish his father had suffered. Cast off after such a distinguished career, thwarted in developing his theories and sharing them with his students, was callous in the extreme. There had to be more behind it!

'And his large body of works, what happened to it?' Jacob enquired.

'They belong to the university and still play a prominent part of the curriculum. So, you see there's not much more to say,' the Dean said, appearing eager to get away. 'Naturally, you have our condolences for your loss.'

'But here's the thing. Although you deemed Morris Barnet superfluous to your requirements, it wasn't the nature of the man to just lay down and die, surely you can appreciate that!'

'To what are you inferring?' the Dean replied, maintaining his stance.

'Simply, there would have been dozens of other takers

for a man of his undoubted academic influence. It's just a pity the faculty he loved were denied access to any additional work he'd have produced after he left these shores,' Jacob continued.

'Are you suggesting that you're aware of the existence of such works?' the Dean enquired, the concern clear in his tone.

'Funny, you should bring that up!' Jacob said, holding up the manuscript. 'Left to me along with his other bits and pieces. Here, you can take a look, if you want.' He tossed a bound copy at the desk, a few feet away.

The Dean feigned a high degree of concentration perusing the piece as if it were for the first time. The difference was <u>they</u> only had a rough first draft, whereas this appeared to be the completed work. It had all started to go wrong when the son no one thought existed burst on the scene with the obituary, which merely exposed the university's callousness, disregarding that it was a policy decision by the powers above not to extol the virtues of the maverick professor to whom they had felt beholden for far too long. More seriously, Jacob Barnet's presence threatened to scupper his plans to keep the university afloat. The number of places that remained unfilled since Barnet's departure wasn't envisaged. Begrudgingly, he and the rest of the trustees had underestimated the degree of influence the man wielded, far beyond his own specialist area, which was why they desperately needed to make up for the shortfall in income. The six-figure advance for the exclusive publication of Morris Barnet's completed works was now seriously in jeopardy and with it his job as Dean of the university.

'As you would expect, we're quite well aware of the

essay,' the Dean said attempting to underplay the situation.

'I've little doubt of that. Even I know this little gem would be the culmination of years of work to come up with something like this,' Jacob replied, sensing he had the upper hand.

'Naturally, we would expect you to submit the work to the university. After all, there's no question as to who owns the rights.'

'That's a little strange since my father obviously didn't see it that way,' Jacob replied, now realising he had a fight on his hands, instead.

'Since there appears to be an impasse, it'll be down to our lawyers to convince you where the property truly belongs. Now, I must get to a meeting,' the Dean said, gathering up his things. He was just about to make a quick get-away when, Jacob said, 'I think <u>that</u> belongs to me!' He pointed to the manuscript that had been conveniently placed under a pile of student's projects.

'Purely accidental,' the other person said, devoid of any contrition. A moment later, he strode out of the room, leaving Morris Barnet's last work on his desk.

Jacob left shortly afterwards. Now everything had fallen into place. The absence of an obituary and prior dismissal was nothing other than a cynical ruse by the university to get its hands on his father's *Magnum Opus*, to which, it appeared, it would go to great lengths to secure, giving him good reason to believe that, in addition, there was a great deal of money at stake. Suddenly, he recalled Jane French's friendly advice about a lawyer. Deducing that Robson Charles owed him a favour for the mess they made over his father's estate, it was opportune for them to make amends, he thought, keying the number into his mobile. A moment later, he heard James Cameron's voice at the other end of the line.

'Jacob, it's good to hear from you.'

'Don't suppose there'd be anyone who knows a thing or two about the ownership of a piece of academic work?' he said, coming straight to the point.

'If you're referring to Intellectual Property, that happens to be my area of expertise,' the young lawyer replied.

'In that case, I may have something for you,' Jacob replied.

'Always happy to oblige but I have to warn you in advance, these things can be quite expensive!'

'Which is precisely why I've come to you, bearing in mind the splendid job you did last time around, if you remember?'

There was a momentary pause on the line.

'I assume you're alluding to the unfortunate mishap over the estate.'

'Hole in one! Let me know if you're interested,' Jacob replied.

'I'm sure something can be worked out. Let me have a word with a few of the partners and I'll get back to you, if that's agreeable?'

'You mean that old fella, Robson?'

'Actually, Charles has retired since we last spoke,' the lawyer divulged.

'And not before time,' Jacob quipped.

There was no response.

'Look forward to speaking again soon,' the person at the other end said, before ending the call. He certainly wasn't prepared to breach the firm's confidence. The truth was, however, they had only just managed to escape calling on their professional indemnity for what amounted to gross negligence over the Morris Barnet Estate. It was a unanimous decision by the partners that Charles Robson was a liability the firm could no longer suffer. Not that the senior partner had gone quietly. Accused of having the rug pulled from under his feet, it had taken a substantial severance package and the assurance his name would still appear on the note paper for him to go off to his cottage in the Cotswolds, where he couldn't do any more harm.

*

The next morning, Jacob had barely finished his breakfast when his phone pinged with a new message from the young lawyer, inviting him to attend lunch at their offices. He couldn't help smiling at the contrast in tone from the previous terse like summons, as if it were an attempt to salvage their reputation.

11

Jacob entered the university, this time accompanied by his legal representation. Although he'd initially opted to follow through on the lunch meeting alone, he'd finally seen that having James with him would add weight to their position. Although, as it was explained to him, it was by no means certain that they would win if the case ended up in court. The problem was how to attribute the rights of work to which both parties had a justifiable claim. The fact a major part of his father's *Magnum Opus* was only completed after he left the university's employ was deemed, much to his disappointment, insufficient to award him title to its ownership. Fortunately, they had followed up on his suspicion that there was more to his father's abrupt dismissal than was conveniently skated over by the university. A quick investigation into its financial affairs had thrown up an institution censured for unfiled accounts going back many years, which gave the impression it was witnessing great difficulty trying to stay afloat.

'Desperate times call for desperate measures' were the words uttered by the new wily senior partner, an altogether different proposition from his predecessor.

Of course, being served with a writ had the desired effect of shaking up the two-hundred-year-old institution. The immediate response from its board of trustees was so different from the hard-nosed attitude to which he was subjected a fortnight earlier. Their suggestion of an around-the-table meeting to thrash out some sort of compromise only added to his impression that not only were they uncertain of their position but couldn't afford the fallout of any bad publicity engendered by a court appearance.

'So, what's the best we can hope for?' Jacob asked, turning to his brief as they entered the specially designated top-floor room, out of range of the daily routine of the place.

'We're holding all the cards. At least that's the impression we have to give,' the young lawyer replied, proceeding to join the other three males and solitary female already present around what resembled a line of camp-like folding tables pushed together for the occasion.

'Good morning, gentlemen, do make yourselves comfortable,' greeted one of the group, a tall man with an unfortunate squint. 'I'm sure we're all busy people, shall we press on?' the same one said, reacquainting himself with the matters at hand from the thin layer of correspondence in front of him.

'Are we not waiting for your main man?' Jacob enquired.

'If you're referring to the Dean, Richard sends his apologies.'

'Skiving off more like,' Jacob mocked, louder than he'd intended.

'I can assure you it's genuine. Something came up at the last moment,' the trustee stressed, feeling the need to justify himself.

'So, I take it you received the writ on behalf of our client?' James said, taking charge.

The comment set off a series of worried looks around

the table as if they'd been left in the dark.

'Indeed, we have,' the spokesman said with a disapproving glance aimed at his fellow trustees, 'which I have to say we have every reason to contest in the strongest possible terms!'

Jacob, incensed, sprung to his feet.

'First, you get rid of the man and then you grab his masterpiece for yourselves, or was that the plan in the first place?'

'I'm sorry, you are whom exactly?' the kind-faced woman enquired.

'Jacob Barnet, the son these friends of yours didn't expect to suddenly crawl out of the woodwork so they wouldn't have anyone around to account to!'

'Nigel, why is it that we're just learning of this young man's existence for the first time?' she asked, directing her question at the senior trustee.

'Probably just an oversight but it has no bearing on what's at stake,' he said dismissively.

'If that's so, why don't you explain to the lady the reason you refused any obituary to such an esteemed member of your faculty. To add to it, when you were approached by the press, they were thrown out on their ears with not so much as a "Comment!"'

All of a sudden, the sedate atmosphere erupted into a series of noisy recriminations.

James, normally straight-faced, broke into a sheepish grin at the unexpected turn of events.

'If you don't mind, we'd propose a short recess,' the tall man said, gesturing to the others to get off their backsides before making a quick exit himself.

'Looks like you've got them quite a bit rattled,' James

said, not hiding his admiration.

'No more than they deserved,' Jacob replied. 'They've got a lot to answer for.'

'You're making it sound like a vendetta.'

'Maybe I am. But is that such a bad thing?'

'I understand where you're coming from but with a proviso that it might be time to put emotions aside and look at the practicalities of the situation.'

'Surely you're not prepared to throw the towel in already? We've only just got started!'

'Jacob, have you thought what you hope to get out of this?'

He hardly had time to come up with a response when the fractious party filed back into the room.

'Can we assume you've reached a consensus?' James enquired.

'Absolutely,' their spokesman replied, seemingly oblivious to the implacable demeanour of the others, who'd appeared to have resumed their previous stance.

'What we propose is a joint ownership of Morris Barnet's last work, any proceeds of which would be divided equally, after the deduction of any costs, of course. That seems to be more than a generous offer from our point of view.'

'I'll need to discuss it with my client,' James said, appearing to give it serious consideration.

'I shouldn't bother because he's not buying it!' Jacob snapped.

'Mr Barnet, there's no way we're going to get involved in horse trading, if that's your ploy. So, I suggest you talk it over with the calmer head of the person next to you.'

'Nigel, old boy, you seem to be forgetting the fact you're not in any position to dictate terms, simply because you haven't got anything with which to negotiate. Surely, you don't need reminding I'm the only one in possession of my father's last manuscript and the way things are going, that's where it's going to remain!'

The trustee, flushed in the face, started to shake violently and had to be helped to his chair.

'Think the fella could do with a drop of the hard stuff,' Jacob quipped.

'So, what's your preferred solution to the mess in which we've rather found ourselves?' the female trustee asked.

'Now that's the question. Why they didn't give you the job rather than grumpy old Nigel here? We'd be having a pint or two of Guinness down the pub by now,' a comment that brought a welcome round of laughter from all but the unfortunate trustee, who'd fallen fast asleep.

'Here's what we're going to do,' Jacob said, with a flash of inspiration.

'You can have this here manuscript,' he said, holding up his father's last work. 'It'll more than likely fetch a few quid if it's as valuable as you obviously think it is.'

There was a look of astonishment on every face, wondering whether they'd heard correctly or were simply at the receiving end of a cynical stunt.

Jacob received a nudge from the person next to him.

'Are you sure about this?' whispered his similarly bemused adviser.

There was no response.

'In fact, I'd wager the money will come in quite useful in your current situation!' he continued, undeterred.

'To what exactly are you alluding?' shouted the senior trustee, who'd unexpectedly regained much of his poise.

'Don't tell me you don't know. Although, the way this

place is run, it's a surprise the boys in blue haven't turned up on your doorstep with a court order by now!'

'That's simply outrageous!' Nigel Chalfont burst out.

'Not according to the latest bank statements,' James Cameron intervened.

'But they are supposed to be confidential!'

'Then, it would pay to be more careful about leaving them hanging around,' the lawyer added, getting up and handing over the documents to the other side he'd come across purely by chance, discarded in the corridor.

'And you are proposing that we are at liberty to utilise the proceeds of such work as we see fit?' the female trustee enquired.

'So long as that entails a new Morris Barnet Faculty and making a scholarship available in his name. Both should ensure this once famous establishment gets back on its feet, wouldn't you agree?' Jacob continued.

'We could certainly do with filling the numbers that have been severely depleted since Morris...' one of the others muttered, before thinking better of it.

'That seems eminently sensible to me,' the female trustee agreed.

'That's settled then,' Jacob said, the first to get up to leave.

'We'll get something off to you in the post,' a deflated Nigel Chalfont replied.

'I believe its more appropriate for our firm to draft the agreement,' James countered.

'Not suggesting for one moment that we don't trust you, but it does need to be watertight,' Jacob added.

The meeting broke up with a false show of camaraderie by both parties and a reluctant acceptance of the best outcome achievable in the circumstances. The reality was not, unsurprisingly, completely different. Unlike the administrators, who were keen to get back to their respective roles thinking they'd probably got off lightly, Jacob was in no hurry to leave the establishment that for the first time didn't exude a hostile environment. Was it, perhaps, because part of him also belonged here that he felt a sense of attachment? he wondered, looking around the philosophy department, which had now been earmarked for rededication, for a last time.

'Quite a performance you put on in there,' James Cameron said, breaking the silence between them once they left the building. 'Maybe, you should consider making a career of it?'

'Because of my big mouth, you mean?'

'No, just what came out of it.'

'It just seemed the most natural solution and it's what Morris here would have wanted, wouldn't you say?'

'And do you think that's why he'd left <u>you</u> to discover the manuscript?' the lawyer posed.

'I'd never thought of that,' Jacob replied, lightly.

'Anyway, if that was his intention, I'm sure he'd agree you did him proud.'

'The wily old fella! You know you might just be right!'

'Looking at it from his point of view, you were probably the only one on whom he could rely.'

'Even more reason to make absolute sure that slippery bunch don't renege on their commitment.'

'Be assured, they'll be left with no room to manoeuvre by the time we're finished,' James said as they entered Euston Tube station.

'Better still, they'll be paying their share of your fees for the privilege,' Jacob added.

'That's not what we agreed,' the lawyer retorted.

'Sorry, I must have missed something.'

Jacob thought for a moment. All he recalled was that he wanted a concession from the lawyers, not that he expected something for nothing.

'Don't concern yourself, we'll recover the whole sum from the other side!' the lawyer said, disappearing down the escalator.

12

Jacob stood in front of the bedroom mirror hardly recognising the image staring back at him. No one need tell him that he had let himself go. The problem was he'd been unable to break out of the malaise he'd experienced since the showdown at the university. Barely leaving the house except for the purchase of essentials that included the obligatory half bottle of Bell's Whisky, there was no respite from his sense of loss. The problem was that the mission he'd set himself had become his whole raison d'etre. Worse were the recriminations over letting go of his father's defining work, which was why, despite urgent reminders from the lawyer's that he was in danger of jeopardising everything they'd achieved, the agreement with the university still hadn't been ratified. He was aware that by making 'doing right by his father' his sole priority, he was in danger of being left behind, at the end of which all he'd have to show was an allayed conscience. However, he felt powerless to do anything about it.

He suddenly recalled the previous night's dream that left him feeling particularly unsettled. It was his last session with the therapist. The rickety old cabinet, to which he'd given sparse attention, had suddenly grown in stature, and was dominating the room. Next to it lay his father's last work, no longer as prominent but with which it clearly shared a common bond. And then came the therapist with those same words: 'Once the readers had made up their own minds, it was for <u>them</u> to apply it as they deemed fit.'

Pondering on his predicament, that was precisely what he hadn't done himself. More seriously, thinking the legacy was his exclusive domain, he'd inadvertently deprived anyone else access. It suddenly became clear those ancient texts belonging solely to the therapist were nothing of the sort and the fact that the cabinet had *opened its doors* was simply an invitation to discover its contents.

Jacob now understood the connection with his father's last work wasn't at all tenuous. It was the opposite. What the therapist had led him to appreciate was the fact the two were inexorably linked. No longer as close-minded to exploring new possibilities, there was no reason to hang on to his father's last work for a moment longer.

Realising his short sightedness, Jacob rushed down-stairs, picked up the official document that had remained untouched for the last three weeks and, giving it no more than a cursory glance, attached his signature.

After a swift spruce up and an alcohol-free breakfast of toast and coffee, he left the house feeling invigorated and made his way on foot to Marylebone, three miles away.

Striding past the boating lake in Regent's Park, ten minutes later, armed with the agreement, Jacob reached his lawyer's office, his natural exuberance returned and confident he could make up for his error of judgment.

The following afternoon, he received confirmation from James Cameron that the trustees had completed the agreement without any amendments. Fortunately, they hadn't queried the extra clause giving them a three-month time limit to make good on their obligations. As James said, that was proof the university was even more desperate to restore the reputation it had enjoyed at the hands of its erstwhile professor.

Over the next few weeks, Jacob emerged from the shadow of his father. No longer seeking the posthumous approval that had held him back from being his own person, he was now able to move on.

Applying himself single-mindedly to earning a living was long overdue. Bills were piling up and most of the money in the bank had gone on essential works to the property. Relying on the petty cash generated from garage sales comprising most of the former contents, which were deemed surplus to requirements, wouldn't keep him going for long. He was clearly running out of options. Putting the house up for sale was probably the only answer.

Another evening pouring over the likes of Aquinas and Schopenhauer and all the other esoteric philosophers between that comprised the last additions to his father's library, was now far more than an attempt to retrace the former's thought process than it might have been previously. Jacob hadn't yet realised that it was providing the preliminary groundwork for making his own mark.

The next morning, noticing that something was placed in his letter box, Jacob opened a hand-delivered envelope to find his personal invitation to the opening of the Morris Barnet Faculty.

'Jaysus! They didn't exactly hang about, did they?' he muttered. 'I'll only have to get myself something to wear for the occasion!' Later that day, ferreting through a clothes box earmarked for the local charity shop Jacob came across a black evening suit still in its original cover. Further examination was unnecessary to ascertain that it was a perfect fit.

13

Jacob entered the packed ceremonial hall attended by the entire faculty of students and lecturers, some privileged to have had personal exposure to Morris Barnet, the majority of whom, however, had only known of the esteemed professor's reputation.

Thinking he could tag on inconspicuously to a seat at the back, he was caught on the hop by Nigel Chalfont's gesture inviting him to come forward. Seeing that the front row was reserved, Jacob took his seat amongst the other trustees and the Dean, whose relaxed expression belied his earlier fear that his job was on the line.

After a belated eulogy extolling the virtues of its former professor, who took prominence on a wide screen and taking full credit for his Posthumous *Magnum Opus*, which, fortuitously, just happened to fall into their lap, Chalfont gave the floor over to the Dean to give details of the new faculty dedicated in Morris Barnet's name. Emphasising the generosity of the trustees in making a scholarship available to the new undergraduates was met with thunderous applause and flash bulbs from several members of the press, who'd suddenly found themselves in favour, now the university needed all the publicity it could generate.

The room was then quickly prepared for the reception when a posse of uniformed waiters suddenly appeared with trays of food and drink. Helping himself to a glass of sparking white wine, seeing no expense spared putting on such a lavish display despite its perilous financial position, Jacob thought he noticed Jane French chatting with a young male journalist.

'I don't suppose it's worth asking what you're doing here?' he said, going up to her.

'Jacob? Sorry, I didn't recognise you for a moment, looking so laid back and relaxed over there,' Jane replied, smiling broadly.

'Well, I couldn't very well turn up in my jeans, if that's what you mean?'

'That wouldn't have stopped you in the past, if I remember correctly.'

'You're not wrong there,' Jacob replied, unaware that his recent transformation went further than just his outward appearance.

'Quite a turn up for the books, wouldn't you say?' she added gazing around the spectacular 18th-century hall.

'Which bit do you mean?'

'Outcast one minute, then to suddenly be the subject of all this acclaim,' she clarified, focusing on Morris Barnet's life-size image.

'I assume you're not just referring to the press,' Jacob quipped, bringing a snigger from the young fellow, whom, he deduced, was the same one subjected to the university's previous snub.

'And I'd be right in thinking you had more than a little to do with pulling this off?' Jane said, taking her turn to probe.

'And what if I did?' Jacob came back. 'What possible interest could it be to you?'

'Don't you remember our last conversation?'

Jacob thought for a moment. So much had occurred since then, he'd forgotten all about the time she turned up at his house after which everything started to fall into place. The truth was the visit was the catalyst, albeit through a tortuous process, to break out of his father's mould and start trying to establish his own identity.

'Didn't you tell me something about leaving the supplement, which was the reason I hadn't heard back?' he blustered.

'I was actually referring to something else,' the young woman replied, not divulging her disappointment that Jacob hadn't taken advantage of her private number.

'Anyway, just to let you know I've joined a book publisher since then. My department focuses on new up and coming authors, especially those with a good story to tell. I'll come to the point. In my view, it doesn't come any better than this. If you're interested, I'm confident we can offer you something that would make it worth your while.'

'What are you looking for?' Jacob asked, casually.

'Your story, Jacob, from the beginning to where you are now.'

'It'll be a hell of a job,' he replied, appearing to give the proposal a modicum of consideration.

'Which is why we would be prepared to fund the undertaking.'

'Meaning what, exactly?'

'Simply, for each tranche of work, you'd be paid an agreed sum.'

'Sounds like you've come well prepared this time around.' Jacob replied.

'Obviously, there would be certain restrictions, which would be set out in the contract. Look, I've really got to get going. Let me know if you're interested,' the diminutive young woman said and started to wander off to her next appointment.

Jacob spent the following days trying to get his thoughts into some semblance of order regarding a written account of his experience and the form it should take. Although he couldn't pretend that he wasn't influenced by the offer of being paid for his efforts, the first half a dozen chapters were all Jane required to confirm her firm's willingness to proceed.

For the next several weeks, Jacob fully immersed himself in mapping out his tale. Surfacing only for meals, and the early morning workout in a local gym, he tackled the task with gusto. Revisiting his childhood in Ireland, this time around, was something he approached more like a spectator looking back on a period of his life devoid of the resentment which had defined his own early years.

Then, discovering his father and the rich heritage he'd been deprived of, and allowing it to take precedence at the expense of self-preservation, was now dealt with by someone who'd successfully come out the other side but with the acknowledgment that it could have quite as easily gone either way.

Two months later, Jacob had something to show. Deciding against allowing his publisher prior view of his work, he made an appointment with Jane French to present what he'd done in person.

He left the smart Mayfair offices disappointed. The young woman was ill and, in any case, as her PA explained, it would take at least another six weeks before his submission reached the top of their pile for him to receive a response.

One morning, a few days before Christmas, he received a contract in the post and bankers draft for ten thousand pounds, representing the publisher's advance for the completed manuscript.

14

Jacob finished reading the passage he'd selected from his novel in front of a packed audience and made his way over to the display area for the signing. The June launch, at Drakes prestigious book shop in central London, was arranged even before the first editions rolled off the press. *A Time to Move On* had already captured the attention of the literary world with the review copies that turned up on its desk, all clamouring for an interview with the latest author it had already decided was destined for fame.

Just as the last of the stack was taken, a young blonde woman in a long trench coat moseyed over to where he was sitting.

'I hope I'm not too late,' she said, casually.

'Sorry, but it appears we've just run out of stock,' Jacob replied, without looking up. 'I could ask whether there any more copies in the back, if you want to hang on for a minute,' he added, searching out the organiser of the event.

'Surely, you wouldn't suppose I would have come all this way empty handed?' she replied, producing his book from her shoulder bag.

It took a moment for Jacob to identify the soft Irish tone, then,

'Kayleigh!' he exclaimed, clearly startled by the presence of his former girlfriend.

'I thought I might just pass by,' she replied.

'How are you? It's been a long time.'

'Is that one question or two?'

'I'm really glad to see you, that's what I mean.'

Just then, he could see Jane French gesturing to try and gain his attention.

'I can see you're in demand,' Kayleigh said.

'It's just my publisher, she's got a personal interest in making this evening a success, as you can imagine,' Jacob replied.

'I wouldn't have expected any different, so you'd best scribble your name and I'll be on my way,' Kayleigh replied.

'It's nothing like that but there's talk of another novel in the offing,' Jacob explained, signing the copy thrust under his nose. 'How long are you planning to be in London?'

'Well, that all depends, doesn't it?' she said non-committally.

Jacob could only look on as Kayleigh drifted off into the night, none the wiser as to how she'd managed to track him down or, more to the point, the motivation behind it.

*

Arriving home before midnight with the events of the evening playing on his mind, Jacob headed straight to the drinks cabinet and poured himself a large whisky, hoping it might alleviate the feeling of unease. Fortunately, the publisher had put his distraction down to being overwhelmed by the response to his maiden work. The reality was quite different. Kayleigh's appearance had disrupted his equilibrium and he needed to work out the reason. The fact he'd never been short of female company since he'd been in London had never fully compensated for the feelings he still harboured for the fiercely independent apothecary from Co. Donegal.

Ignoring the hour, Jacob tapped the number he still knew by heart into his mobile.

'Hello,' came a tired voice from the other end of the line.

'It's not too late, is it? I just wanted to apologise for not giving you enough time earlier on.'

'That's understandable, you being the main attraction,' Kayleigh said, mustering a reply.

'So, what I was wondering was if we can catch up properly, there's a lot to talk about.'

'Like, why you just took off two and half years ago, deciding never to return?'

'It's a lot more complicated than that,' Jacob hesitated.

'You mean the whole deal about your remorse on discovering your father wasn't the scoundrel you'd been led to believe. I'll grant you it made a good read. I was nearly convinced myself until I recognised the person behind the façade.'

'I can see now that wasn't right, so at least allow me to make it up to you.'

There was a short pause.

'Maybe, another time. There's an offer of a job I'm mulling over here in London but I'm leaving early tomorrow… Goodnight, Jacob,' she said finally, the line going dead before he'd even had the chance to respond or enquire about his mother.

The next morning, Jacob awoke, still fully clothed, on the living room sofa with only an empty whisky bottle for company. He'd obviously lost all track of time. The conversation with Kayleigh had unsettled him far more than he imagined. Thinking he could just skate over that period in his life without any consideration for those left behind was now, he realised, callous in the extreme. The truth was putting it out of his mind as if it never existed was an easier option than making good the void he'd left in their lives.

Suddenly, he found himself transported back into heated discussion with the therapist trying to reconcile the idea of a superior level of understanding with his own predicament. That was then but now he was looking forward to a successful career as a novelist or so he wanted to believe. The truth was he'd conveniently sidestepped taking any responsibility for his past without which, as was explained to him, he couldn't expect to move on. Moreover, in haste to make a name for himself in the commercial world, he'd forgotten about the finer points of his father's *Magnum Opus* which, not so long ago, was his sole reason for existence. There was no doubt he'd been remiss on both counts.

Now he'd received a poignant reminder of his shortcomings, it behoved him to put them right.

First off, putting his follow-up plans to his novel on hold, he moved across to his laptop and purchased a long overdue plane ticket to Dublin. With a bit of luck, when he returned this time, it wouldn't be on his own.

15

Jacob was hard at work putting his latest thoughts down on paper, seemingly oblivious to the attractive young woman's presence a few feet away. The truth was it hadn't been easy getting back to where he left off when the plaudits from his novel were still ringing through his ears. The visit to Ireland, two months earlier, had affected him more than he'd anticipated it would. The foreboding he'd built up in his mind on seeing his mother again, with everything that had transpired in the interim, was replaced with unexpected affection for a frail old woman in a care home. Just the faintest recognition he received in return was enough. But it was the enthusiastic response he gained from the young offenders to the extract from his book, covering his own experience at the same detention centre, which more than anything, left him with a burning desire to continue making a difference.

'You really were being serious,' Kayleigh remarked, perusing the latest additions of reading material that found themselves on the shelves.

'About what in particular?' Jacob muttered.

'Your sudden interest in so called non-wordly subjects,' she said, focusing her attention on a volume of Biblical commentaries. 'Next, you're going to tell me you're contemplating joining the clergy,' she mocked.

'I've learned to broaden my perspective and not to discount anything, that's all,' Jacob replied, finding it hard to concentrate on the task in hand.

'Sounds like a bit of a contradiction to me.'

'Not if your starting point of being angry against the whole world clouded your judgment on everything else.'

'And what brought you to that conclusion, may I ask? I don't recall reading it in the book.'

'If you remember, it's when *Brian* comes to the realisation if he'd been mistaken about his father, the fear it may have impacted on his own life?'

'And that's when he hooks up with that wise old man at the funeral who puts him right?'

'Something like that,' Jacob answered, keeping it as close as possible to his experience with the therapist.

'Then, all that stuff about finding he was descended from a line of illustrious academics, who managed to escape war-torn Europe, seemed a bit improbable, even for you!'

'But that's the point. It's about someone discovering an identity of which he feels he's been deprived.'

'And that's what you've done, is it? Latching on to some random group of thinkers, who, up to recently you never knew existed!'

'Put it this way, it was a start of a process.'

'One of which, I assume, is still ongoing?'

'Why, isn't it for everyone?'

'Only, I'd quite like to know with whom I'm getting involved this time around,' Kayleigh enquired, keeping her distance.

'In your position, I'd probably have thought the same way. That's why I needed to put you right,' Jacob replied, not revealing the valuable heritage brought to him by those old family albums together with the responsibility for it to continue.

'And that you did, turning up at the crack of dawn at Heathrow Terminal One!'

'It was only repaying like with like with you at the launch,' Jacob countered.

'Whatever it was, I suppose it was more than I had come to expect.'

'And why you had absolutely no hesitation succumbing to my irresistible charm,' he added, turning around to face his girlfriend.

'Probably against my better judgment. At least my parents detected a change from the scallywag of old.'

'That's what I've been trying to tell you these past weeks,' not needing reminding he'd still plenty of convincing to do.

'As I said, I'm prepared to give it a try and see how things work out,' Kayleigh said non-committally but with a smile indicating otherwise.

'As long as you can keep putting your stamp on the place, you mean,' Jacob quipped gazing around at the newly fashioned study she'd instigated.

'Just get your head back down to your writing, otherwise I'll be late and I'm the only one dispensing today,' Kayleigh retorted, gathering up her things and then moving briskly away.

Jacob glanced over at the same editions that had caught her attention. The fact he'd unconsciously begun to replicate the contents of the therapist's display cabinet had initially been for research purposes for the next book in the series. That there was too much to cover in the first one was blatantly clear from early on. But there was far more to it than just correcting an injustice he'd skated over previously in that his protagonist was mirroring his own experience almost as it unravelled. Although, the prospect of joining the same religious order was probably a step too far, he could see the attraction of a life devoted to loftier ideals.

Where the story would take him next, he was unsure; even less whether it held the same commercial value for his publisher. Strangely, it didn't seem to matter as much.

Epilogue

North London Cemetery

The middle-aged man in a dark fedora respectfully entered the burial ground, carefully dodging small craters there to hinder its visitor's progress. Closed for many years except for the few individuals yet to take up their reserved plots, it was hardly a surprise the early 19th century cemetery had fallen into disrepair to the extent the inscriptions on whole generations of headstones lining the route could only be deciphered with extreme difficulty.

It wasn't altogether inconceivable that amongst them were those, which at some time or other, had belonged to him. Not that he was in denial of who they were or that they were best forgotten. On the contrary, he'd come to realise they were an essential part of life's bumpy trajectory.

Jacob put up the collar of his raincoat. He could never fathom why, even in the middle of summer, the temperature at these places seemed to be regulated at a completely different level. It had to be more than just being exposed to the elements that gave it a permanent chill. Perhaps, that was sufficient reason for most people to make a quick getaway once they'd paid their respects, eager to return to the land of the living, as if they were to hang around too long, they might somehow be courting their own fate.

Yet he had a different take on the subject. Far from a

reminder of his own mortality, each visit to these places provided a testimony of the several lifetimes that had already made up his own span of just shy of two score years and ten, none of which at any stage, if he was completely honest, he could have ever predicted. Surely, life's greatest gift was that of *not knowing*. It was perhaps inevitable, given his inability to comprehend the bigger picture, that it had taken all the challenges life had thrown at him to gain that appreciation. Hadn't his own experience shown that believing he was in control of anything other than the most perfunctory aspects of his life proven to be folly?

Proceeding along the well-trodden path he'd taken on several previous occasions, he came to a halt a few minutes later at a grave set apart from the rest.

The simple inscription on the newly commissioned headstone said everything about the man for whom he continued to feel a deep affection.

Although, they hadn't been in contact for many years, the therapist was never far from his thoughts. That had all changed with the call he received out of the blue, six weeks ago. Not that there was any inauspicious reason for their prolonged absence.

At first impression, little had changed about the modest abode in which he himself once enjoyed an extended stay, other than that it was now filled by a kind female carer and that age had naturally taken its toll on an individual now well into his eighties, nothing else seemed particularly awry.

After the briefest exchange of pleasantries that preceded coming together of any two close acquaintances after such a long period, the therapist wasted no time getting down to business. Intent on going over every detail from the very first time their paths crossed to the strides, he, Jacob, had subsequently taken in his life, including the fact he now had a family of his own to carry on the Barnet line, there seemed no ulterior motive for their particular union.

It was only when the therapist revealed that his condition was terminal that he realised that the process was a test of his worthiness and the other person was simply laying the ground to relieve himself of a burden which, up till now, he hadn't felt sufficiently qualified to reveal.

Learning there was more to the casual association with his father than he was led to believe was no great surprise from the odd comment the therapist was inclined to let slip from time to time.

However, it was the fact Morris had entrusted Simon with the task of *bringing his son back*, he now appreciated was due to the special relationship which had obviously existed between the two. But it went a great deal further. Morris hadn't left anything to chance to the extent the therapist was not only privy to his father's final work but was likely to have been the main proponent behind its spiritual dimension. It was, therefore, no accident Morris had placed its intended use in the capable hands of his confidant.

The whole episode was a carefully prepared strategy executed with the precision of a highly accomplished individual. The fact the therapist relied upon him, Jacob Barnet, to make the first approach and then in all the hours talking over his various issues, only ever laying the seed, allowing the patient to make the running, was testimony to his expertise.

And then, that last time when their roles were suddenly reversed and Simon opened up, revealing he was widowed many years before, describing how the tragic loss of his only child had left him bereft of any family and thereafter, open to the charge of hiding behind the mantle of a therapist. Most meaningful of all, however, was Simon saying the benefit he received from their relationship had gone a long way to filling the void left in his own life.

Remaining a short while longer in contemplative prayer, Jacob gathered up a few pebbles and placed them on the marble headstone in keeping with the traditions he shared with the special individual he had come to visit.

Comforted he'd at least been able to make up for the shortfall in respect of his own father, Jacob made his way back to his car, stopping to wash his hands to rid himself of the negative forces inclined to attach themselves after a bereavement.

Checking the time on his watch, he needed to get a move on for his afternoon class at the university. The fact the Morris Barnet Faculty had welcomed him with open arms was as unexpected as the following his novel's journey of identity had established amongst its young fraternity.

Most relevantly, writing had provided the commercial means to eventually change course. Further works ensued paralleling his own life's experience, which, in truth relied more upon an existing reputation rather than on any merit for broadening his audience. However, it was the recently published *An Abraham Moment* which encapsulated the deeper meaning of everything he'd gleaned at the hands of the therapist.

Heading towards central London, the seed had already been sowed with his father's *Magnum Opus*; he was merely following on by making it his own.

THE END

THE REVIEWS ARE IN!

"I appreciated how well the author described my kitchen. Have you seen it? I recently added a lazy Susan to hold my appliances in this blind cabinet. So the way it works is that the lazy Susan is on rails, and you mount the rails to the cabinet shelf, pull out the lazy Susan, and voila! You can access the back region of the cabinet! I put my seldom used appliances back there like the dehydrator. It's useful in the summer when I want to dry fruit for baking, but I don't need access to it all the time. Have you tried one of my new oatmeal gargoyle cookies? I started a limited edition series for the cookie truck. There's been a line 30 people deep for these! I won't tell you the secret ingredient...but you can guess. Go on, guess. Oh, right, you haven't had one yet! Anyway, yeah, the book is great. Gus is a real rascal." — Brant

"These guys are awesome. The book captured the dance club atmosphere really well. I kind of wish we'd seen that bar, though. It sounds dope. I hear it's based on a place in Toronto? That's wild. Anyway, that weird little dog is cool, too. We had a killer time in Multnomah. Definitely will come back." — Patrice

"Everyone keeps asking me questions about Gustopher, the little Tomme de Savoie! I am as in the darkness as the rest of you! Where did he come from? Je ne sais pas. How old is he? Je ne sais pas. Did I know him from before? Ah bon! Now you are in the fascinating country! Who can say...who can say? I do think that the author was cruel in her description of me, though. A little touch of malice on her part. It's not as if I didn't help the boys along with my hints. I just know that when Gus gets bigger — La vache! I was not supposed to tell you that!" — Remi

"Gustopher is extremely cool, and I am happy I got to meet the little one right away. The author did a great job describing his first words! I am getting choked up just remembering it. I do wonder if it will stay teacup-sized, though. Because if Gus is going to get bigger, it's going to be hard to find clothes." — Xavi

"Listen. I know in my gut that those freaks work for The Volcano no matter what they claim, but I have to say, I respect their attack strategy. They have access to arson weaponry, they laid down some great cover fire with that fire-lizard-type creature. You know who would be really interested in that kind of firepower? The military. Maybe I should make a call. Excuse me." — Captain Angry Ballet Dancer

"I feel REALLY drawn to the bi-colored eyes on that little bearded dragon. I didn't catch the name, but I thought I heard them call it Gus? That's one cute kid, let me tell you. Maybe I should try and get in touch with them, see if they need any help." — Big Black bouncer at dance club, The Golden Knight

"*burbling, growling noises*" — Gustopher

"I mean, this book did a decent job with the guys and that little possum thing, but I noticed that she really didn't describe the bachelorette party or the bride and groom very well. There was a LOT more to that story. Let me fill you in. Okay. So the CRAZY thing about this wedding, right, is that I actually met Brandon FIRST, way before Holly ever met him. And he liked me first, because, you know, he has good taste, and we actually got serious for a while. But like, suddenly he wasn't as into Jell-O shots and paintball and Steven Seagal movies anymore, because Holly comes along with her progressive polyamory ideas, (big whoop) and cool art festival stories and suddenly, Brandon had gotten with her! I mean, the nerve! So anyway —" [review cut short by arrival of police] — Bachelorette No. 6